This book is dedicated to
MAUDIE, **B**ARCLAY,
MANDU
& **L**AIKA

Лайка = Laika
pronounced like+(a)

First U.S. edition 2013

Library of Congress Catalog Card Number 2012950622
ISBN 978-0-7636-6822-8

TWP   18 17 16 15 14 13
10 9 8 7 6 5 4 3 2 1

Printed in Johor Bahru, Malaysia

This book was typeset in Eureka Sans.
The illustrations were created digitally.

TEMPLAR BOOKS

an imprint of Candlewick Press
99 Dover Street
Somerville, Massachusetts 02144
www.candlewick.com

Picture credit: page 32
photograph of Laika
copyright © Keystone/
Getty Images

templar books
an imprint of Candlewick Press

Laika was a stray
wandering the streets of Moscow.
She had no family and nowhere to call home.

Laika was all alone.

At night she looked at the stars and made a wish—
to find a family who would love her.

Then someone
noticed Laika. Because she
was on her own, he thought
she would be perfect for
a very special job. . . .

A group of scientists wanted her to try out their new spacecraft. She trained very hard and had to pass many tests until finally . . .

Laika was ready to go into space.
She climbed aboard her spaceship and waited.

10 ... 9 ... 8 ... 7 ... 6 ... 5 ... 4 ... 3 ... 2 ... 1 ...

The whole world watched as little Laika zoomed up toward the stars.

Now everyone knew Laika's name, but as her spaceship circled the earth, she felt more alone than ever.

Then her rocket started making funny noises.
Something had gone wrong.

5:08

Back at mission control, the screens went blank.
Laika's rocket no longer showed any signs of life.

Everyone on Earth thought Laika was lost,
so they wrote books about her, made stamps with
her face on them, and even put up a statue of her.

Laika, the astronaut dog, whose journey into space
paved the way for people to follow,
would never be forgotten.

But Laika was not lost at all.
Laika had been found.

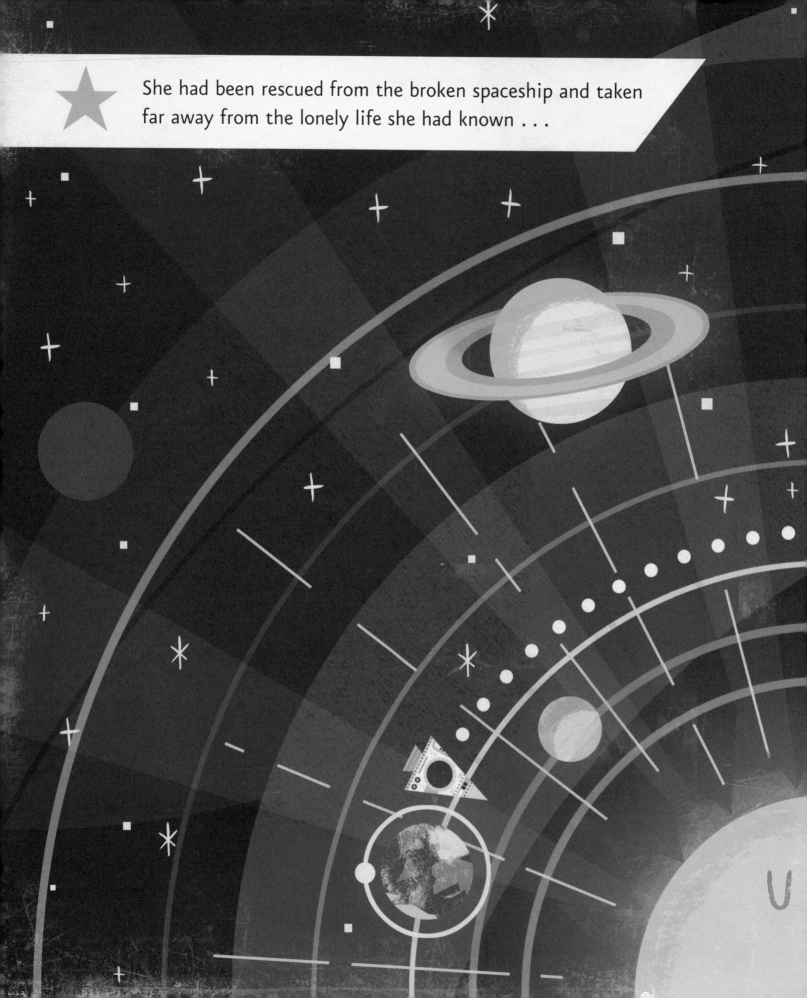

She had been rescued from the broken spaceship and taken far away from the lonely life she had known . . .

by a loving family
that she had always
dreamed of finding.

A note from the author:

On November 3, 1957, Laika became the first
animal to orbit Earth when she was launched into
space in the *Sputnik 2* rocket.

A few hours later, Laika's spacecraft malfunctioned.
Though many think Laika perished, this story,
with its happy ending for the brave little dog,
is the one I choose to believe.